Ainity

DANICA PECK

FROM THE AUTHOR OF BATTLES OF AZRIEL SERIES

Amity

DANICA PECK

Amity

Published by Ouroborus Book Services via IngramSpark
www.ouroborusbooks.com.au

Cover design by Dayna Watson
contact.daynawatson@gmail.com

*Dedicated to everyone that walked away,
thank you for setting me free.*

Prologue

There is a swing set in my back yard.

It sits behind the pine trees, overlooking the fields. Nicholas stands behind me, pushing the swing. I move my legs with the wind, willing myself to go higher. Silver hair flies across my face and butterflies do flips in my stomach with each fall.

He catches the swing, slowing it to a halt. I tilt my head towards him and note the smile he gives me. He is well practiced in the art of charm. I can't say the same for myself. I step off the swing and turn to face him, leaning forward and resting my hands on the seat of the swing.

I notice his eyes. Grey, like mine. Blank and unclaimed by fate. I think he is beautiful, in every sense of the word. His angelic face is the reason that every girl on the island, including me, fantasises about him.

Nicholas leans forward, his face close to mine. He closes the space between us and plants a soft kiss on the corner of my lips. I close my eyes at the touch. The softness of his lips on my skin makes my skin flush. I open my eyes as he leans back and smiles at me.

"Catch you later, Winters," he says, before turning on his heels and walking up to my house.

My fingers linger on the spot he kissed me. A smile forms. I replay the memory in my head, scrunching my nose at his use of my last name. I can't recall him ever saying my birth name.

I skip up to the back door and Mum appears in all her grace and beauty. I am envious of her strawberry blonde curls. My hair has no volume whatsoever.

"Perhaps Nicholas will be your bond mate," Mum says in her not-so-subtle way of saying she saw the kiss.

"I hope not," I say as I feel myself redden, which isn't hard as I am usually snow white.

Mum asks me why I say that.

I look into Mum's golden eyes.

"He is a Lex," I state blankly.

"His parents are from the Lex Tribe," she corrects me.

I roll my eyes.

"Come inside for dinner, Amity," Mum says with a shake of her head. "Your father just got home."

I follow Mum into the kitchen where I find my sister with her nose in a book. We look similar. We're both petite with Mum's fair skin and Dad's silver hair. Sierra hasn't bonded yet either.

Dad sits down at the table, despite the fact he is covered in dirt and sweat from working the farms all day. It is the duty of the Terra Tribe, my parents' tribe. The men work on the farms and the women grow herbs and make medicines and such.

It is a simple life, and the one I hope to live.

Chapter One

I am from a world that isn't like yours. Thira is a world where choice is taken from you. There are four tribes. Terra, which my parents belong in. Lex, which Nicholas's parents are. Piscator and Bellator. And me? I don't belong to any of them.

When I bonded my eyes changed to purple. The island I am from doesn't even have a name for it, we just call those with purple eyes *abominations*. I remember trying to read into it before I bonded but there were no details about it, just that any person found with purple eyes will be outlawed or sentenced to death.

Not liking either of those options, I ran. I got on a boat and got as far away from the island as I could. For seven years I have lived on another island so insignificant that it doesn't possess a name, and has only one living resident apart from me.

For seven years there has been a heartbeat in my chest that wasn't mine. Not an actual heartbeat, but a phantom one I suppose. I can feel everything that my bond mate feels. I can hear every chaotic thought; I get pulled into every dream and relive every memory that he does. No matter how far I run, I can't escape them. These things I feel aren't mine.

As I lay asleep, I dream though my bond mate's eyes. Wesley stands at the foot of his bed, mirror on the wall. I see a surly Lex man enter his room, his father, though his eyes are bloodshot, as though he's been crying. Lord Mason wears a black suit with a green tie – the Lex Tribe's uniform.

Their tribe is the ruling system of Thira. Their values are truth and justice. They are the law, the judges and the executioners.

"Wesley, sit down," Lord Mason says as he sits on the edge of the bed.

From the mirror's reflection from the other side of the room I can see that Wesley's eyes are grey.

Lord Mason falters his words, lost to what he needs to say.

"The Bellator Tribe returned from a hunt this morning."

The word hunt is used loosely, it is more of a scout of the island, ensuring its safety. The Bellators are the protectors of the island.

"Dad?" Wesley asks, his nerves rising. "What is it?"

Lord Mason looks at the wall, unable to look at his son. I notice the photos of Nicholas and Wesley on the mirror, even a photograph of me remains.

"It is your brother," Lord Mason says, having found his voice. "His body was found in the woods."

There is a split pause in the bond, a moment for what is said to register and process. I wake up, my chest in physical pain. Throwing the blanket off me, I jump out of bed and run out of the house. I run up the hillside til I reach the top, a cliff face to the ocean.

Screaming out in pain, I fall to my knees. Tears cascade to the ground. Lucian, the other resident on this island and my guardian, comes and sits down beside me. He holds his gaze over the ocean and lets me cry my eyes out.

How could this happen?

I feel like a kaleidoscope of emotions. I feel my heart break at the loss of the boy who gave me my first kiss, the first person I ever loved, and despite the fact it's been seven years, I still remember the feeling as though it was yesterday. I also feel confusion, our last moment together was so awful that I feel the smallest bit of relief, which makes me feel sick to my stomach.

Wesley, poor Wesley. His pain crashes down on me like a wave on a beach. It is overwhelming, his pain more than anything that I can bear and all my thoughts are on myself. Guilt and sadness consume me until I begin to feel numb, empty, a void in the darkness.

Managing to stop crying, I fall back and sit down, swinging my legs over the edge of the cliff.

Keeping my eyes trained on the waves below, I tell Lucian what I saw in my dream.

"Will you be returning home?" he asks in a raspy voice. I look into his tunnel black eyes. "Remember, I don't need a bond to know your thoughts."

I lean my head on his shoulder, for emotional support, not comfort. He has too much muscle for this to actually be comfortable. I tell him that I will return, that my trip home won't be for long.

"Does he know?" he asks. I lift my head from his shoulder and look at him, confused. "Does your bond mate know that you love his brother?"

Shaking my head, I turn away from Lucian and look back down at the ocean. My eyes find the boats that float on the shoreline. There are three little boats, all of which Lucian has enchanted to return to this island. So, I will have to sail myself to Thira, but the journey home will just require me to sit in the boat.

"Does it ever get better?" I ask, looking at Lucian.

He turns to me and asks, "Does what get better?"

I place my hand to my chest, and bite my lower lip, suppressing the urge to cry again.

Lucian places his arm around my shoulder.

"It has been over ten years, and there are still moments that I miss her. The pain isn't constant anymore, it is more like waves. It comes and goes."

As I look over the ocean in the direction that Thira lies, a funny feeling residing in me.

"I have a feeling," I say, focusing on the line where the sky meets the sea.

Lucian asks me what kind of feeling.

"That this trip is going to change life as I know it."

"In a good way or bad?" he asks.

"Both."

Lucian removes his arm from around me and stands up, offering me his hand which I accept. He pulls me to my feet and embraces me in a hug.

"Come back to me," he whispers into my hair.

Lucian saved my life when I first ran away from home. I crashed my boat not far from here and he rescued me and nursed me back to health. I've lived here ever since. He is a father figure to me.

Releasing me from the hug, Lucian and I walk back to the house. I need to pack a bag and head back home; back to an island where I am not welcome, back to where I will be called an abomination.

Chapter Two

The bond is quick and unexpected. It is that feeling of leaning back on a chair and almost falling. It is overwhelming. It was with the person I least expected as well – Wesley, the brother of the one I actually loved. That morning, I had been running away from the Mason property in the Lex Tribe part of town. Tears clouded my vision and I slammed into Wesley, falling to the ground. He offered me his hand, his fingers stroking my wrist gently before he gripped my hand firmly, pulling me to my feet. As I offered him thanks, I met his gaze. Purple bled into the grey, changing his eyes, our eyes.

She is so beautiful.

I could hear his voice in my head. I dropped his hand and clutched my chest, his heartbeat echoing over mine. The rush of his emotions hit me like a brick wall.

That feeling of hitting a brick wall with a rush of emotions is how I feel right now as my boat reaches the island and I see Wesley standing on the beach. My stomach wrenches as I jump into the shallows and drag my boat up onto the sand. Wesley is staring at me, shock written all over his face. He is pale, much paler than I recall. He runs his hand though his hair, as though lost, unsure what to do. I notice his handshake as he brings it down to his side.

I open my mouth to say something, but words don't form. I don't know what to say, and even if I did, it wouldn't satisfy what he needs to hear.

His thoughts echo in my head as though they are my own.

What is she doing here? Did she sense my pain over Nicholas? Her eyes are still purple. Have they always been? What will the town say? Why can't I hear her thoughts? It'd be much easier knowing what she is thinking right now. How has she kept that from me? We are bonded after all.

Wow, I forgot how beautiful she was.

Slowly, as though approaching a frightened animal, I take a step away from the boat and towards Wesley. I meet his gaze, as though asking for permission to take another step. His shock of seeing me wears off and he runs over to me, and picks me up in a twirl. He lowers me back to my feet and as I go to speak, he kisses me. My whole body freezes, my heartbeat races a million miles an hour in my chest. Nerves and confusion consume me and I know he feels it all. He takes a step back and looks at his feet, muttering his apologies. I suppress my emotions like Lucian taught me, but Wesley's are overpowering.

Shit! Fuck! I just kissed her! She's going to leave again! Why would you do that? Fucking idiot! Just apologise. Again!

"Would anyone notice if I sleep in the town stables?" I ask, stopping myself from asking the question I actually want to ask. "I recall them being pretty quiet and not much people traffic."

His heart drops. I feel it as though it is in my own chest. He steps towards me again, puts his hands on my arms and his forehead to mine. I close my eyes and hold my breath. I can hear the battle in his mind, his urge to blurt out that he loves me. He hesitates long enough to stop himself. Releasing me, he takes a step back again. I open my eyes and let out a sigh of relief. Looking at him, his skin is flushed. Walking past him, I enter the trees and follow the path down to the stables. I hear footsteps behind me and know that Wesley is following.

It is only a short walk from the shore to the stables, when I come out of the trees and into view, I keep my head down so people don't notice my eyes. I walk past two teenagers standing in the doorway. I glance up and see a black stallion in the end stable. He paws the ground when he sees me. I walk down to him and hold my hand out cautiously. He presses his nose to my palm; I step forward and throw my arms around the stallion's neck.

He was Nicholas's horse; he was also the horse I learnt to ride on.

"I miss him too." My throat feels swollen.

"Is that why you came back?" Wesley asks from behind me.

I release the stallion and turn to Wesley. I wince when I see that his eyes are no longer grey, but purple again. He notices the change in my emotions and apologises for his question.

"It's not that, it's your eyes," I say softly, looking down at the floor. "They've gone purple again."

He puts his hand under my chin and pushes, making me look up at him. He then puts his hand into his back pocket and pulls out a pair of sunshades, which he puts on. I laugh.

"Don't tell anyone I am here, please," I ask. He promises to keep it quiet. I bid him goodnight and he leaves the stables.

The stable beside Nicholas's stallion is empty, so I walk inside, closing the gate behind me. I sit in the corner, pulling a long shirt from my backpack, using it as a blanket.

I close my eyes and drift off to sleep.

I stand in the town square. All the streets are empty. I see snow fall from the trees to the ground.

Behind me, a voice that sounds like Wesley says, "Choose."

"Why?" I question.

"Choose," he repeats.

I glance over my shoulder, but no one is there. I look forward again.

"Choose!" yells Wesley's voice.

"NO!" I demand, standing my ground.

A wolf appears a few yards ahead. It crouches low and stalks towards me. Its lip peeling back as it snarls, baring its white teeth. A growl gurgles within its throat as it prepares its attack.

I think about running, but if I act like prey, it will act like the hunter. The wolf lunges at me and instinct takes over. My hands go up and magic flows from my fingers and hits the wolf. When I look over at it, the wolf is gone.

I am alone.

I turn and see Nicholas walking towards me. He calls me *baby* like he used to and something stirs in my stomach.

"Did you know it was Wesley who killed me?" he whispers before pressing a finger to his lip. He turns away and I call him a liar.

Facing me again he shouts at me. "Why are you protecting him? You promised to avenge me!"

Chapter Three

I wake to a sweaty body, with my hair clinging to me and a pang of guilt and confusion in my chest. I am lying on the stable floor, but the morning sun slips in a ray of light from the ceiling. I see Nicholas's horse looking over the stable wall down at me. I listen to the voices outside to see if I recognise any. If I do, I will have to run. But none sound familiar.

I sit up and wipe my face with my hands. There was something weird about that dream I just had. Why do our minds speak in riddles? I wish our subconscious would just tell us instead of giving us bizarre dreams and unnerving feelings.

I bring my knees to my chest and bury my face in them. I wish I had stayed on my island with Lucian. How could I return and curse Wesley back to his fate?

As the minutes pass, the details of the dream begin

to fade. I have to run my hands behind my neck, beneath my hair every few seconds as the sweat collects.

What if I learnt that Wesley really was involved in Nicholas's death?

Would I be able to avenge him if that were the case?

I don't think I could. Plus, to do so would end the Mason family name.

My mother told me once that my father was disappointed that she didn't give him a boy. He loved my sister and I, but girls don't keep the family name, and even if we did, our children are given our husbands' names.

The stable door opens. I raise my head and watch Wesley enter. He looks nervous and pale.

"You might want to leave the stables," he says. "It's my father, he is on his way down to the stables to take Phillip for a ride."

Phillip, that was the name of Nicholas's stallion.

"Now?" I ask.

Nervously, I touch my forehead. I push myself up from the floor and keep my eyes down as I walk out of the stables, whispering thanks to Wesley as I pass him.

Abomination.

That is what Lord Mason calls people like me. If he found me out, I wouldn't make it off this island alive.

Chapter Four

I decide to go see my family. If they learn I am in town, my mother's heart would probably break at me not visiting her. As I depart the stables, I steal a pair of sunshades that are sitting unattended. I don't want to be revealed.

I walk in the middle of the road. A road I haven't walked in years but still remember as though it was yesterday. There was a sense of home, walking this route again. I notice the town's people staring at me, some are neighbours I remember, others strangers. I hear their whispers.

Is that the Winters girl?
How long has it been?
Do you know why she ran away?
Why is she here?
What is her name again?

As I walk through the Terra Tribe as an outsider, I remember how glamorous I used to find it. The homes are little townhouses, and the farmlands begin behind the homes. It is a simple lifestyle, but I can't help but love it, I always have. There is no vanity, no conflict.

Until me.

If I reveal my eyes to my parents, they will forsake me.

Permanently.

"Amity," someone calls. Her voice velvet and familiar. "What drags you back to our little island?"

Waiting for the voice to catch up, I am reunited with my sister. When she reaches me, she embraces me in a hug. Awestruck, I hug Sierra back. When she releases me, I look her over. Her once long hair is now curved around her chin. Her once unclaimed eyes, now a piercing green.

When I left, she was eighteen, two years older than I and her eyes were not claimed by fate. Sierra blushes slightly when I ask her who she bonded with, making me admire the green of her eyes even more.

The answer she gives throws me. Tahlia Remington was a fair and beautiful girl from the Bellator Tribe; well, her parents were. She and Sierra now belong to the Lex Tribe. The ruling tribe of our island. Sierra is well-suited to the Lex Tribe – she was always the brains of our family, her nose forever stuck in a book. Tahlia however was that girl who was always climbing trees or focusing on her target practise. I'm surprised she didn't stay in her own tribe. But fate never gives us a choice I suppose.

Hiding my shock, I exclaim my congratulations and ask when. Sierra's face falls. It happened three years ago. Many things happened in the past seven years, she points out, and for all that time no one knew how to reach me. There is even a 'we thought you were dead' speech, not that I don't deserve this lecture but she could have waited until we reached Mum and Dad's. Then all three could preach the same words of disappointment to me.

We reach our parents' house much quicker than I planned to. I twist the bracelet around my wrist as a nervous habit. It has a purple band and a reflective crystal. If I tilt it right when I look at it, I can almost see my purple eyes.

Sierra reaches forward and opens the door, calling out to our parents as we step over the threshold.

"Amity!" Mum exclaims, as she rounds the corridor and sees me. Tears form in her eyes and she steps forward as though to hug me but then stops and just asks me, "You're back? Are you all right?"

"I'm fine."

I look around our house. Dad stands behind her, giving me a strange look, like I am a different person than the daughter he knew. He isn't wrong.

Mum ushers us all into the living room and asks me to take my sunshades off before she disappears into the kitchen to fetch us all drinks. I try to smile as I sit on the couch across from the one Dad sits on. I don't remove my glasses.

Dad just stares at me, doesn't say a word. I whisper that I'm sorry because that is the only word I can muster. Mum returns and places drinks in front of us all, again asking me to take off the sunshades. Again, I ignore and just thank her for the drink and take a small sip.

"Where have you been?" Dad said, making everyone, especially me, tense. His golden eyes staring at me from under his reading glasses, eyebrows drawn together so that a crease had been drawn between them. His silver hair has gone almost white since I last saw him.

"Honestly," I say. "I don't know exactly. An island a few hours from here. I never asked for the name."

"All the rules you have broken, we demand an explanation. What was so important that you had to leave?"

The room is silent, even my sister's breathing beside me is so faint in sound.

His eyes stay on me for a few more moments before he looks away and curses, and orders me to remove the shades.

It is on my mind to argue, but never have I raised my voice to my parents, especially my father. With a final attempt to hide them, I look down as I remove the shades. There is a heartbeat pounding in my ears, this time my own. The fear to look up is overwhelming, but when I finally do, the silence is deafening.

Without a word Dad stands up. Mum puts her hand on his arm as though to calm him. He doesn't even look at me and demands that I leave.

The urge to jump up from my seat and demand

he understand and accept me as his daughter raises its head, but I suppress the words and stand up, not meeting Mum's eyes, as I know she is looking at me. Sierra stands up and shouts at Dad to defend me, saying all the things I wanted to say, but he silences her.

There is nothing to be said. Without looking at any of them I walk out of the house and slam the front door behind.

"FUCK!" I shout, taking a deep breath as my mind replays what just happened. I am so frustrated with myself; did I expect anything else? Did I expect to return home and have my parents welcome me back with open arms? If my own parents couldn't accept me, no one in this town will. I honestly don't understand why I even came back. I miss Nicholas and hurt over the fact that he is dead, but why did I return? I haven't seen or talked to Nicholas in over seven years and the way we left things meant we had no place in each other's lives anymore. Why am I here?

I remember the swing, the kiss, our first kiss. I remember the boy I loved, the boy I needed to say goodbye to.

As I step away from my parents' house, I drop the shades to the ground and accept my sentence as an abomination.

Chapter Five

The walk I take back to the stables is full of people staring at the colour of my eyes. Do they fear me, pity me or despise me? A ring of sunlight burns into the clouds and over the trees.

I follow the whispers all the way down to the stables.

Is that the Winters girl?

Her eyes are purple!

Is that why she ran away?

What does purple mean?

Is she dangerous?

She is an abomination!

The stables are crowded when I arrive, but people move out of my path as they notice my eyes. I settle back into the corner of the stall I slept in the night before. I close my eyes, needing a moment.

"Purple suits you," says my sister from the stable gate. Forcing a smile, I look up at her. She opens the gate and slips inside.

"If it makes you feel better, I'm pretty sure Dad is sleeping on the couch tonight," Sierra says as she walks over and sits beside me. She tells me how after I stormed out Mum turned on Dad for kicking me out, that I probably ran away because of the fear of their rejection. Apparently, Dad flinched at that accusation, though I can't imagine my father flinching. He was always so composed.

"I asked Tahlia if you could stay with us," Sierra continued. Before she finishes her sentence, I already know that the answer was a no. If the Lex Tribe caught them out, they would be shunned.

"Who did you bond with?" Sierra asks.

The question sets off warning bells in my head. I want to tell her, but I don't know how to. I feel sick at the thought of lying to her, but if I tell her it is Wesley and Tahlia finds out, who is to stop her from telling the town and having Wesley cast out?

"Just imagine that fate didn't choose the colour of our eye," I whisper, changing the subject, my eyes still looking straight ahead. "Imagine if we chose the tribe we wanted to be in, chose who to love, despite the tribe they chose for themselves."

Sierra laughs and tells me that I am dreaming, and even as a child I always had an active imagination. I ask her if she could have chosen for herself, what would she have done? I turn to meet her gaze; our eyes linger for a moment.

She turns away. Is she ashamed in her answer?

"I would have still chosen the Lex Tribe, but I wanted to be with Nicholas Mason, rather than Tahlia." Nicholas? I'm shocked, I never realised she also had feelings for him, and she was obviously oblivious to mine for him. "Don't get me wrong," she continues. "I love Tahlia, but until the bond joined us, I never considered or even knew I could be turned on by another girl."

She asks me what I would have done. Simple. Terra Tribe and Nicholas. Although I don't tell her the Nicholas part, just that no one had caught my interest yet. That is when she asks again who I actually did bond with. It's a question I cannot answer.

Sierra turns to me and I feel she is about to argue, but she purses her lips and sits back, choosing not to be pushy, and instead she changes the topic.

"Talking about Nicholas, have you heard he died?"

As she says it, it sets in how real it is. I feel my heart drop in my chest and my eyes go to my hands, my right thumb running the nail across my left palm, a weird habit I do when I am awkward or trying not to let my emotions show.

I can feel Sierra's eyes on me, studying my reaction.

"That's why you're back?" Sierra questions. "Isn't it?"

Nodding, scared if I speak, knowing she would hear the break in my voice. I ask her with a slight beg in my voice if we can talk about something else.

We move to lighter topics. Sierra tells me about her relationship with Tahlia and the work they do in the

Lex Tribe. I tell her about Lucian and survival skills he has taught me.

The sun sets faster than expected. It is dark out as Sierra leaves the stables to return to her home and wife. The lights in the stable come on and I hear Wesley's voice call out to me.

There is something in the stable with us.

I jump to my feet and run out of the stall. Wesley sees me panicked and asks what is wrong. From across the stable corridor I hear a wolf howl, summoning the rest of the pack. But I see nothing there. I pull a small knife from my boot and throw it in the direction from which the howl came. I hear a yelp and the thud of a body. Fear courses through me, not of the wolves; I've fought wolves before. What scares me is that wolves don't exist on this island. Especially ones you can't see.

Racing toward the barn door, I pull the door shut and lock it, quickly surveying all the stables to ensure no other points of entry.

Wesley again asks me what is going on and where those wolf sounds are coming from and what did I throw my knife at. Wesley's fear and confusion floods into me, blocking my concentration. I try and listen for footsteps of more wolves, but Wesley's heartbeat in my ears deafens me to all other sounds. As I open my mouth to answer, all the lights in the barn go off. We hear something trying to get inside. It sounds like it is throwing itself at the door to break in. I remember all the stable staff I heard throughout the day, walking past the stall I'd sat in with my sister, I hope they've all gone home for the night so I won't have to keep them from the danger.

I run back into the stable I was squatting in and retrieve my weapons from my bag. I wrap my belt and sword around my waist, throw my quiver of arrows over my shoulder and retrieve my compound bow.

As I walk out of the stall, I start explaining to Wesley that we need to get outside so whatever is out there doesn't get in, but I am cut short when I hear whinnying from the horses outside. Nervously, I ask Wesley how many horses are currently out there.

Wesley shrugs and mumbles something that I don't understand.

"Why aren't they all in the stables?"

"There are more horses than there are stables, some of them stay in the paddocks out front."

The banging stops, and we both stare at the door and listen. It remains silent. I turn to Wesley and tilt my head to the door; he nods, understanding my meaning. We run to the door and open it enough to slip out before locking it behind us. The lights out here are still on so I step forward into the centre of the illumination. Wesley follows in suit. He asks in a hushed whisper if I can see anything. I shake my head as I listen to the soft growls surround us. I see the shadow of a wolf but not the creature; retrieving an arrow, I take aim to where the body should be. Releasing, I hear a whine and body fall. The growls turn into howls and barks. Cursing, I reach for another arrow.

"What the hell is out here?" Wesley shouts just

before he screams in pain and is thrown to the ground.

Aiming the arrow a few inches higher than Wesley, I release and sigh in relief when I hear another whine.

"Unseen hounds," I reply while listening intensively to the sound of paws and growls circle us.

Two paws hit me square in the chest and I'm thrown to the ground. Winded for a moment. I ignore the fact that it hurts to breathe and reach for a knife from my boot. Once I retrieve the knife, I plunge it upwards and hit my target. Scrunching my nose in disgust, I push the invisible body off me.

Another wolf, and I hear the paw prints scurry off into the night. I roll onto my stomach and look over to where I see Wesley investigating a scratch across his thigh. Pushing myself off the ground, I ask if he is okay. When he signals that he is, I instruct him to follow me back into the stables. I open the barn door and usher him in first, glancing around to ensure there are no spectators. I see no one, though surely someone must have heard us. I close the door behind me when I enter.

As Wesley limps over to a chair on the far wall, I rummage through the storage cupboards and find the medical kit. Removing it from its shelf, I take it over to Wesley, kneeling down before him.

"Would you like to tell me what's going on, or should we wait for more ghost wolf things to eat us?" he asks as I pour alcohol over a cotton cloth.

"I believe they are unseen wolves. There are cultures on other islands that worship and live amongst wolves; they have the ability to bring back the alpha wolves' spirits when they die," I explain, not meeting his gaze. "The thing that confuses me is, those islands are on the other side of world. I don't understand how they came here, or why."

He winces as I press the cloth to the scratch across his thigh. He questions my knowledge of cleaning his wound.

"I had to learn how to survive, being on my own," I say as I continues to clean the scratch. "I picked up a few skills over the years."

As I check that I've cleaned the cut thoroughly, I tell him how I met someone who has taught me how to survive on my own. I try not to meet his gaze because every time I see his purple irises looking back at me, I feel guilty. For returning I have cursed him to his fate. He is lucky he hasn't been noticed yet. People will talk eventually if he keeps the shades on. He puts his hand below my chin and forces me to look up at him, and as he does, he leans down to kiss me. His desire floods through me. It is intoxicating but it isn't mine. I pull back and he frowns in frustration. I stand up, holding the medicine kit to return to its home as an excuse.

Chapter Six

I train my eyes to the floor after I return the medicine kit to its shelf in the cupboard. Wesley is Lex-born so has the habit of arguing his point. It's the reason our leaders are always in strife, too many alpha personalities demanding their way to be correct.

"Fate put us together," Wesley demands as he stands up.

Biting my urge to shout, I reply that fate isn't always right and that I don't want to talk about this. He walks over to me and I look into his eyes. They glow slightly and I feel mine glow back in response. I wonder what it means. Is it because both our emotions are running high perhaps?

He whispers my name, softly, almost seductive. His lips almost touching mine, his eyes look down at my lips as he whispers that he is in love with me. I want to die inside, him saying those words out loud is like someone stabbing me in the chest. His lips softly press against mine and I close my eyes, allowing him to kiss me. He pulls me to him and the kiss turns from soft to passionate. His lips move down to my neck and he tugs my shirt collar aside to kiss my collarbone. My mind instinctively goes back to seven years ago.

Nicholas is on top of me. He is heavy, but he isn't squashing me. He is kissing down my collarbone as he tries to unbutton my shirt. I push his hands away and try to bring his focus back to my lips. I enjoy kissing Nicholas, more than enjoy it, but I am not ready for more. I ask him to slow down but he kisses me to silence me and follows by whispering in my ear that this is what we have to do if I want to be with him.

He finishes unbuttoning my shirt and starts kissing down my chest.

"You do want to bond with me, don't you?" he asks as I pull the blanket over to cover myself. He unbuttons his own shirt and I am suddenly conflicted; his chest is covered in lines that shape and chisel him, and a great urge rises in my to kiss that chest. He pulls off his pants and I return to questioning if I am ready for this step.

Blinking away the memory, I push Wesley off me. When I meet his gaze, I realise that he saw it, too, thanks to our bond. Rage floods though the bond; for a moment the pain of the loss of his brother is smothered.

"Is that why you left?" he asks. "He fucking raped you? I thought you left because you didn't want to be with me!"

Shaking my head, I insist that it was because our eyes turned purple. Wesley silences me by shouting at me to stop lying. I defend Nicholas by muttering it wasn't rape but I'm too ashamed to meet Wesley's gaze as I say it. When I look up, he is just staring at me with shock, like he doesn't know what to say. He asks how old I was, and states that I was still a child and that Nicholas was an adult that manipulated me. I wince as he shouts rape again. Begging him to stop talking, I press my hands to my face, the memory haunting me, I just want to forget.

"It wasn't rape," I insist, lowering my hands and meeting his eyes. "And you have to understand, I was in love with your brother since I was nine years old. And just because he used and manipulated me, unfortunately it doesn't erase six years of feelings."

"How long?" he asks. I look at him, confused. I don't understand what he means. "How long after did we match?"

I train my eyes back to the floor, my mind remembering the morning after. I had woken up alone, naked, bruises between my legs. I felt ashamed, dirty. I was filled with guilt, it made me feel sick to my core. My body felt defiled. I quickly retrieved my clothes and went to leave the room, but as I passed the window, I saw Nicholas in the street flirting with another girl. It made me want to scream, watching him stroke a strand of hair from her face and place it behind her ear. He did that to me on countless occasions. It was this moment I realised he never wanted to bond with me. I felt sick to my stomach and ran out of the house using the back door. I was unable to face him. There was a pathway through the forest that led close to mine. I cried as I ran so I didn't notice Wesley and crashed into him. When our eyes met, I saw the grey turn to purple.

Wesley storms out of the stables, his emotions suffocating me. His anger at fate for bonding us the morning after his brother took advantage of me, hatred at the brother that he should be mourning.

I remember the photo he has of us in his room. It was taken at one of Nicholas's birthdays. I was dressed as a fairy princess and Wesley as a pirate. It was captured at the right moment; I was laughing at something he had said. We were only thirteen or something in this photo but I wonder, if we had bonded here would our eyes be a different colour? Was it because of what Nicholas did to me the night before that we were cursed to be abominations?

Wesley finally calms down, wherever he is; that or he finally finds a way to server our bond. I walk to his parents' home. Since the town thought he was unclaimed by fate he would still be in the family home. I am careful to stay out of sight of people; if I'm caught entering his home after being so careless with my eyes, he will be caught, too. When I reach his home, it's only his bedroom light on, which means his parents must not be home. I break in the back door and walk up the stairs to his room. I knock but he doesn't answer. I open the door and close it behind me, leaning on the door as though I can't stand without it. He apologises but I brush it off and look at him. For the first time since I arriving, I truly look at him.

He and Nicholas are so similar in facial features,

but where Wesley is tall and rather slim, Nicholas had been chiselled with a larger build. Wesley asks how long I am staying for and I stop my mind from comparing the Mason brothers. I tell him I am leaving straight after the funeral. I was originally planning to stay longer but I need Wesley's eyes to change back to grey.

He lowers his head at my answer of leaving so soon, and I know he dreads the thought of never seeing me again.

I whisper my own apologies and turn to leave the room, but as I open the door, he says my name. I pause in the doorway but don't look back at him. He asks me if I ever loved him. I look down, unsure how to answer. Do I lie to protect his feelings or tell the truth to allow him to move on?

I tell him that I didn't and without looking back, I leave.

Chapter Seven

It is the morning of the funeral; the whole town is gathering in the cemetery whilst I still stand in the stables. All dressed in black and unable to move, I am in mixed conflict. Did I not come here to say goodbye, to avenge him? Sierra has told me it was a freak hunting accident, but I have a nagging feeling that's a cover up.

I needed to say goodbye, but in this moment, I feel unable to attend, fear rooting me to the spot. I look to the floor and my eyes fixate on an ant that runs around a piece of grain. The dress I wear falls to the floor loosely, tight up around my stomach and chest then falling freely from my waist and split up my leg. It was terribly uncomfortable, and not something I would usually wear, but considering I have nothing in my bag of weapons that is funeral approved, I'm grateful to Sierra for lending it to me. I dread seeing my parents almost as much as I fear seeing Nicholas's body. His lifeless body.

"I always knew you wouldn't be in Terra Tribe," says my mother's voice. I look up and see her standing before me. Her auburn hair almost glowing in the sunlight. "It suits you, the purple."

I repeat what she first said as a question.

"You were always an adventurous child. You were too wild to be in Terra. You were too unique to be in Lex. Never in my wildest dream did I think you would be purple."

I look away from her and ask if she knows why purple eyes are an outcast. She replies that she doesn't and asks if I would educate her on the matter. I return my gaze, unsure if she is ready for the truth, but unable to tell her I look away again.

She steps forward and takes my hand in hers; I look at her and am comforted in the fact that she is looking into my eyes without fear.

"If the town turns on you today, I will step in. You are my daughter. The colour of your eyes doesn't matter to me; I will always protect you."

I start to cry and she pulls me into a hug, whispering her apologies into my ear. I melt into her arms and never want to let her go. I feel as though a weight has been lifted off me; she accepts me. My mother accepts me. My heart is spinning in disbelief and my heart is doing summersaults. We break from the hug and I wipe the tears from my cheek and tell her my thanks.

She leans in and plants a kiss before turning to leave, saying that she has to find my father and join him at the funeral. I close my eyes and let the fear fill me before letting it disperse. As I leave the barn, I feel like a child leaving her home by herself for the first time. When I reach the cemetery, I see Wesley standing before Nicholas's body which is laid upon a wooden table. It is tradition to burn the body, as that is how fate reclaims the soul. I see Wesley's mum indicate for him to remove his shades. I tune into him and hear him say that he can't allow the town to see him cry. It is a good cover but how long can he get away with wearing his shades everywhere? The town will grow suspicious eventually. His father pats him on the back, and puts his own shades on. He is the Lord of this town; he won't show weakness. The whole town weeps for their fallen prince; well he wasn't a prince, but he was the heir to this town, especially if his eyes turned green like his parents.

Wesley is searching the crowd and I know he is looking for me, and I lean against the tree far away enough from the people to not draw attention. He tilts his head as though to invite me to come down to him, not even seeming nervous that I wear no shades and my eyes are clear for all to see.

Slowly, I push away from the tree and start walking towards the crowd, towards Nicholas. My chest feels heavy, nerves consume every inch of my body but I stay on the path. I don't know what scares me more as I walk through the crowd, the fear of what the town would do, or seeing Nicholas's body and saying goodbye. The whispers are like a beehive. Coming from all angles.

That is the youngest Winters daughter.

When did she come back?

Are her eyes purple?!

Monster!

An abomination!

No wonder she ran away.

What is she doing here?

I reach the wooden table where Nicholas lays. My fingers linger on the edge and I resist the urge to lean forward and press a final kiss upon his lips. I gaze over his body. There are no injuries, nothing, he looks fake. I want to scream. I want to cry. I want to go back in time seven years and get over my jealousy and not run out of his bedroom.

Lord Mason hisses at me that I'm not welcome, grabs my arm and pulls me away from his son. Wesley goes to step in but I shake my head at him, willing him not to get involved.

"Please elaborate why that is, my Lord," I snarl. As I look up to meet his gaze, I see him flinch. "Or is it solely because of the colour of my eyes?"

He calls me an abomination and demands to know why I returned to town. I try to form a lie but nothing comes to mind.

"Because Nicholas was her bond mate!" Sierra shouts from the crowd.

I turn to my sister, trying to hide the confusion from my face. I glance to Wesley and he looks as shocked as I feel. Lord Mason releases my arm and takes a step back, asking me if it's true.

I nod, shocking myself and everyone in sight range. He shakes his head and states it must be a lie because Nicholas's eyes aren't purple. I explain that when I ran away it tampered with our bond, turning our eyes back to grey.

"If this is true, once we burn his body and his soul returned to fate, your eyes will change back to grey. Until then we must contain you."

Wesley steps between me and his father and, as politely as he can around a sensitive subject, asks why purple is an abomination. Lord Mason falters, he has no answer. No one does. It is a superstition. Purple is rare. Rare is unknown. The unknown is dangerous. That is how this island works. Before Lord Mason could form an argument to state I am dangerous and remind everyone that I'm an abomination, wolves howl in the distance. Thunder follows the howls and I look up at the grey skies. More howls follow. Many more than the night Wesley and I faced them. This is the whole pack. The beehive of voices gets louder, but this time the words aren't about me, it's confusion over the wolf howls they just heard. Many of the crowd rush from their seats and flee the funeral from the opposite direction, while many of the Bellator's stand and turn towards the sound, curiosity getting the better of them.

"Well my Lord, you are about to find out what purple means," I whisper, looking in the direction the howls are coming from.

Chapter Eight

A lot of the horses aren't in the stables and when I hear them whining, I know that is where the wolves must be heading. Without a second thought I take off towards the stables. I stumble, and have to take off the heels Sierra leant me and throw them aside. I continue running, as fast as I can. I can feel the material of my dress at my ankles and a fear of tripping entered my mind. As the stables come into view, the body force of something unseen crashes into me and I fall into the dirt. I groan in pain as I roll over and push myself off the ground. I can hear the creature growling but I can't see it. Storm clouds gather, creating an unnatural darkness and I know the other wolves weren't far behind. I hold my hand out as I remain standing in a crouch position. I can feel the wolf's hot breath on my hand.

Wes, Sierra, my parents and Lord Mason catch up

to me. I hiss at them not to move as I slowly take a step back.

Lord Mason curses under his breath and snaps that there is nothing there.

I see the creature's paw print deepen in the ground. Preparing for the fact it is about to pounce, I throw myself to the ground but his front paw still scratches against my arm. I scream in pain. Not having a moment to hesitate, I kick out and know I hit my target when the wolf whimpers then growls.

"Wesley!" I call out, not taking my eyes off the paw prints forming a circle as the wolf loops around me slowly. Attempting to scare its prey, me. "I need you to retrieve my sword!" Wesley takes off past me towards the stables.

I question if I am the reason these wolves are on the island, if I am the prey? It still makes no sense as I've never crossed anyone from these islands before. I glance back to ensure my family is away from the danger.

The paw prints pause for a moment as though it wondering whether or not to change targets. I take that moment to lunge at it. Lucky for me, I have a small knife in my bra so I pull that out in time to jam into the wolf's shoulder. However, not before its jaw takes hold of my arm. It clamps down, breaking skin, and I gasp in searing pain. I pull out my knife from the wolf and thrust it forward, the knife slicing into the wolf's throat. When it shudders its last breath, I free my arm, now bleeding from the bite.

I tear a strip from the bottom of my dress, killing

two birds with one stone – my dress now shorter and easier not to trip over and a bandage to tie around my arm. My teeth pull at the material, to tighten it around my bicep.

From the stables, I hear Wesley call out. I run to him and find him outside of the stables, my sword in front of him and the door shut behind him. When he sees me, he throws the sword in my direction. I run forward and catch it, slashing at the space in front of him. Another wolf falls and Wesley let out a sigh of relief.

As the wolves surround us, I think things couldn't get worse. What a jinx that always is. Without fail, it begins to rain.

I curse under my breath; the rain makes the soil wet. Which means soon we will no longer see the wolf's footprints.

This is the moment of truth; I stand beneath the lights out front of the stables where at least a dozen wolves surround Wesley and me. I see our parents at the top of the hill staring down at us and the stables. What I am about to do is going to save Wesley and me, but it will also see me sentenced to death by his father.

Keeping my eyes on my family, I drop my sword. Sierra takes a step forward but our father grabs her arm, halting her. I raise my hands up to the lights and focus on the energy particles within them. As I summon the light, the glass bulbs shatter and what looks like a million fireflies fly down toward my hands. I pull my hands back past my shoulders then throw them forward, releasing the light particles.

When they find the wolves, they attach themselves, allowing me and everyone else to see them. They look mystical, golden and glowing. I retrieve my sword and slash at the wolf nearest to me. Quickly counting, there are nine wolves left. Knowing they are now visible, the growls increase and they attack me more quickly, but this is what I have spent seven years training for. While keeping my movements graceful, as Lucian trained me, and Wesley calling out timed locations of the wolves, I have all nine of them killed within minutes.

As I stand amongst the bodies, the light particles begin to fade. I hear footsteps, and raising my head I see my parents, my sister and Lord Mason walking their way over to me.

"What was that?" Lord Mason demands as he reaches Wesley and me.

Wesley steps in, defending me and reminding him that I have just saved their lives.

"Doubtful!" he snaps at his son. "Those things were probably here for her!"

Wesley explains to his father that he was attacked by these wolves the other night also, not mentioning the fact I was also there when this happened.

Before Lord Mason can speak again, my father interjects and asks me what he has just seen. Our eyes meet and he doesn't flinch or look away. He is curious.

"Magic," Sierra states, stepping forward. "Purple means magic, its why it's so rare."

I nod. When Lucian first found me, he quickly discovered that purple meant magic. It was an important part to why I had to learn to control my emotion. Magic is so easily connected to them. I was a fast student, he used to tell me. I excelled his training and tested the laws of magic.

Lord Mason is silent for a moment, as though lost for words. "I see," he says when he finally speaks. "Amity Winters, you are exiled from this island."

Wesley and Sierra both protest but he raises his hand and shouts at both of them.

"This is my town! MY RULES!"

Sierra opens her mouth to argue but I shake my head, stopping her. She doesn't have to get exiled with me. Wesley reaches for me, but I step out of his grasp.

He frowns at me and through our bond I tell him not to get caught. His hand instinctively goes to his face, checking that his sun shades are still on. They must be annoying to continue wearing in this rain. I take another step back, sword still in hand.

"And what will you do, *my Lord,* when these wolves return? You can't see them. They go for strength, and since this is your town, it will be your funeral next week."

Having not stepped back far enough, Lord Mason backhands me. The sound of his hand to my cheek echoes. Without another word, I look back at him and smirk. Turning away, I walk to the stables, pulling the door open and entering. I grab my belongings, pack them onto Phillip and mount him. I ride him out of the stables. I take the time to look down at Lord Mason. Sierra and Mum both smile at me. I turn to my father and see he looks sad. I smile at him, trying to indicate that I am not mad at him in any way.

Wesley runs over to me on Phillip. He begs me to stay, saying he will reason with his father. I shush him and lean down.

"I will return tomorrow night; this isn't over. Something or someone is on this island. Those wolves are an abomination."

Sitting back up straight on Phillip, we take off towards where I left my boat. I look back at my family and wish I could have said something.

Chapter Nine

There is a storm brewing as the boat comes to a halt in its port. I jump off the boat into the shallow waters and start running in the direction of Lucian's house. He must see me coming because he is at his front door when I reach the top of the hill.

"What are you doing back so soon, child?" he asks as I reach the front door.

I tell Lucian that I was exiled. He summons me inside and ask me to explain. I tell him everything, from my parents to Wesley to the wolves. I explain what happened before I left. He looks away from me and into the fireplace, going over what I just told him. His brows crease together.

"You said the wolves were completely invisible, right?" he questions. "But when you threw light particles on them, you could see them?"

I nod, standing from the couch to retrieve water from the kitchen. He is confused, explaining that it isn't possible. Unseen wolves are spirits, but since the light attached to them, they can't be what I thought.

I ask what that means, as I sit back on the couch.

He takes his gaze from the fire and looks at me.

"It means that there is someone else on that island with purple eyes."

I tell Lucian I just need a moment to myself and walk out of his house and back up to the cliff edge. It has to be Wesley; he has purple eyes which means he can access magic also, if he tries. I can just see the island from here. A dark, threatening storm cloud circles it. The waves below me crash loudly against the cliff. I close my eyes and use our bond to see Wesley. He is in the stables, but he isn't alone.

There is a slim girl with blue hair walking towards him, slowly clapping her hands. Her eyes catch my interest, one red, one blue. That is even rarer than mine. Her body is slender, and the dress she wears hangs loosely and covers almost nothing.

"You had one job," she says, lowering her hands after a final clap. "The girl in exchange for your brother."

Wesley remains silent, his eyes glued to the floor despite the occasional glance at this girl. He finds her breathtaking. She clicks her tongue as though impatient and bored of this visit.

She stands inches from him and tells him that purple doesn't suit him. I have the urge to slap her, shame we can't do that through the bond.

"Have I ever told you about my eyes?" she asks, turning away from him and placing distance between them.

He shakes his head indicating he hasn't when she turns back to him. She smiles, her teeth white and straight. She bites her pink lip as though building suspense.

"You see, fate gifted me with two lovers. The first was a man of the ocean, he gave me the blue eyes. We lived on another island not far from here. But I was bored. Then I was approached, given a way to break the soul tie, break the bond. I faked my death, and to this day he doesn't know I am alive."

She walks over to Wesley and stands close to him again, her lips inches away from his. "When I came here, I met your brother, and he with his body and his lips... there is no love in our bond, just lust."

As she speaks, her eyes flutter down to Wesley's mouth.

"Shall we make your bond mate jealous?" she whispers, her lips just touching Wesley's. "Perhaps that will bring her running back."

This time she kisses Wesley and he doesn't push her back. His heart races in his chest, but then it drops in disappointment when he feels me through the bond, that I'm not fazed by the kiss, my thoughts all on the girl kissing him and wondering who she is. From the stable doors a newcomer clears his throat. The girl turns around and smiles at the man that now walks over to them. His eyes are still grey, unmated. His brunette curls are a mess and he wore tight black clothes outlining his figure.

"Did I hear you let the girl leave?" the man says as the blue-haired girl steps back from Wesley and wraps her fingers within the newcomer's.

"Karlson," Wesley says, nervousness hidden in his voice. "Ella was just criticising my lack of dedication to the job."

Karlson reaches into his back pocket and pulls out a small journal. Wesley takes it, muttering his thanks but frowns when he realises that he can't open it.

"She has spelled it so only the girl can open it. You will give it to her, and do not fail this time."

Wesley looks from the journal back to Karlson, and asks what *she* has in store for me. Karlson and Ella turn to each other, sharing looks. You can tell they are loyal to each other as well as this mystery woman.

"We aren't sure," Ella says, dropping the superior voice. "We think it has something to do with the fact she has purple eyes."

As Ella goes to say something else, Karlson hushes her and states she has said too much. He tells Wesley that it is crucial I receive and read the journal, then they both turn away and walk out of the stables, leaving Wesley alone with the journal he couldn't open.

Chapter Ten

The sky is darkening, as though some force of nature is attempting to snuff out the light of the world. The waves below crash violently against the cliff. It sounds like thunder. A maddening idea is playing in my head, but my feet are rooted to the ground, preventing me from taking the step.

"Amity!" I hear Lucian call as the rain starts to fall.

It is warm, which is confusing to my senses. Rain always looks cold. But I find it freeing. It washes away everything; a clean slate. I hear Lucian shout my name again but it is too late. The madness has won.

I look up at the sky and take a step off the cliff. When I go over the edge many things happen. My heart feels like it stops in my chest from the overload of fear. A scream forms in my throat but no sound escapes. The air forming around me makes it near impossible to breathe, though that could just be the fear as well. Despite my urge to shut my eyes, they remain glued open. The butterflies in my stomach are in chaos. My ears dread the sound of waves crashing below. My nervous system prepares to hit the water. I manage to take a breath in as I crash beneath the surface.

The water is calmer below the waves. It's ice cold, attacking my skin like a million tiny knives. I wait. The lack of oxygen making my head fuzzy. My body fights the urge to breathe in but I resist, knowing it'll just be water that fills my lungs if I do.

There is a moment of doubt. Perhaps I made a mistake in jumping. Before my eyes, a light appears, a golden light of warm energy that looks like a million fireflies. It floats towards me and into my chest. It shows me Nicholas. He is smiling at me, his charming devilish smile. His eyes are red.

"Find him," a deafening voice echoes around me.

In my mind I protest that he is dead.

The voice echoes the same command to me.

The light vanishes and my eyes struggle to readjust to the darkness underwater. My lungs feel like they are on fire, craving oxygen. I start kicking and using my arms to swim to the surface. The moment I break the surface and breathe in the air, a wave crashes into me. I am thrown below the surface again, my throat burning from the saltwater I swallowed. My body reacts and tries to cough up the water, but whilst I'm still under it just causes me to swallow more. Fear consumes my chest like a black hole as I fight back to the surface. I gasp for air once I am above water. I notice the cliff face and attempt to swim against the waves but another large one hits me and drags me back under. I swim below the current and around the cliff towards the beach. When my lungs begin to burn again, I swim to the surface. I let out a breath of relief to see I made it out of harm's way of hitting the cliffs. Before I have a chance to catch my breath another wave slams into me, thrusting me forwards. My body hits sand and I sit up, relieved to find myself on the beach. I'm on all fours, coughing up the water I swallowed. I look up, eyes squinting, stinging from the saltwater. I see the blurry outline of Lucian running towards me. His legs splash through the water.

"Foolish girl!" he curses as he leans down and offers his hand. "What in fate's name were you trying to do other than kill yourself?"

Accepting his hand, he pulls me to my feet. My throat is raw and scratchy as I try to speak.

"I needed to speak to fate," I say between coughs. "I wanted to know how to break the bond between Wes and I, I felt that Fate owed me that much."

Lucian looks at me, stunned. After he recovers from his initial shock to my reasoning for what looked like a suicide attempt to him, he asks me if it worked.

"No, but she told me how to find Nicholas," I tell him, feeling conflicted over what I have learnt, the selfish part of me wondering if Fate would give me the answer I seek if I found Nicholas. But how could

Nicholas be alive, I question. I saw his body at the funeral.

"Does that mean he's alive?"

He is asking the same question that I am.

Chapter Eleven

The island is quiet when I arrive. Too quiet. As though no life inhabits it. The trees are just visible in the moonlight. I sail to a beach far from the town to avoid detection, as I am, after all, still exiled. The waves wash upon the shore like a soft lullaby. I exit the boat and pull it up onto the shore. I am listening to the silence. On edge. The hairs on the back on my neck are raised. An owl hoots in the distance and the wind rustles the leaves but as far as I can tell, I am alone. Where are the Bellator hunting parties? Hand on the hilt of my sword, my boots sink into the sand with each step I take towards the trees. I rub my arms to rid my goosebumps as I walk into the trees and find a clearing. Sitting with my back against the tree and my bag and weapons between my legs, I have my knees up to lean my head and arms on them.

I close my eyes and listen to Wesley's heartbeat. It is steady, even. He must be asleep. It becomes a comforting sound, like a safety blanket and I doze off to the beats.

The dream world claims me quickly. I'm back in Nicholas's bed. He kisses me and moves his hands down my body. I grab his head to stop it and he takes my hands and pins them above me.

"You said you wanted to save me," he whispers in my ear.

He goes to kiss my neck but I thrust my knee into his groin and he rolls off me in pain, releasing his grip on me. I jump off the bed and run to the door, pulling it open.

Wesley stands in the door frame, a glowing wolf at his side. I scream to warn him but he tosses me aside with a flick of his wrist and sets the wolf on Nicholas.

I jerk awake.

The sunlight is bleeding through the trees. I stretch my arms above my head, and my back cracks in protest at my sleeping position.

I am unsure how to get into town to retrieve the diary. I am beyond curious to know who these strangers are and who they work for. I also need to find Nicholas, because from what fate said, I assume he is still alive. But if that is true, whose body did I see at the funeral?

I hear laughter and wolf calls. Throwing my bag over my shoulder, I cautiously make my way towards the sound, down towards the beach. As I get closer, I hear the splashes of people running into the waves.

"I thought you'd return to the stables?" Wesley says, appearing behind me, making me jump. As my heart and nerves take a moment to return to normal, I explain that I can't be seen. I ask how he found me. Perhaps I need to find a more secluded place to make camp. Wesley explains he looked into the bond – apparently I haven't learnt to close off my mind as well as I thought, or perhaps Wesley can still peek in because of the bond.

"Where is the diary?" I ask.

He opens his mouth to ask how I know. I tap my fingers to my temples and he groans, frustrated. He berates me for spying on him when I ask for the diary again. I see it in his jacket pocket, so without a word I reach in and despite his protest, I take the diary and walk into the forest without turning back.

Chapter Twelve

I sit within the trees, not far from the stables. It isn't the best hiding spot but I want to hear any commotion that goes on in the town. Plus, I half expect Wesley to tell his dad I am back, just because he's mad at me. I open the diary and look at the messy handwriting. Only the first half of the pages are written in. The back of the diary is blank.

I flip back to the first page and read:

Adrian and I bonded today; it was mixed feelings. I was so happy it was him as we have been best friends since we were children, but our eyes changed to purple. That makes us outcasts. If our parents learn the truth, they would have us murdered, so we left. We packed our bags in the middle of the day and disappeared into the forest. In the far corner the highest cliff on the island is empty to humans. We're building a house using tools we've stolen and the materials the forest offers us. It is just us in our own little solitude.

*Lucky we both come from the **Bellator** tribe, it allowed us to be trained in survival. We know how to hunt, build fires. As long as no one comes looking for us we will be fine. But being here with Adrian, there are things I'm missing back home.*

I miss my little sister and our bedroom forts we'd make to have girl conversations.

I miss my father teaching me how to hunt.

I miss my mum, brushing my hair.

And I miss that boy from Lex that I would fool around with whenever Adrian and I would fight. He was delicious.

As good as the sex is with Adrian, I occasionally needed that extra satisfaction that Nicholas would give me. But now I can never go back.

The sun is setting, and Adrian is calling me inside to him.

Nicholas? Does she mean Nicholas Mason?

I wonder how I don't remember this girl. I can't even recall hearing about her but I must have – two people from the island just don't go missing without there being talk. I am proof of that. I turn to the next page.

We are fucking like three times a day, mostly to pass the time. We've made a good little routine. We wake up, we fuck, we hunt, we make a fire and cook what we've caught, we fuck, we go to the waterfall to bathe, we explore a bit, return to our almost dying fire, spark it up again, eat the remaining food, we fuck again and then sleep.

As much as I love Adrian, it's kind of lonely with only him as company.

The next few pages I flip though, she goes on about hunting skills and how bored she is. I stop about ten pages in when it starts getting interesting again.

Adrian is starting to act weird. I catch him talking to himself. And the last two mornings he has been outside with a fire before I even wake. Even last night, he went straight to bed after dinner, not even a kiss goodnight.

His currently outside, and I can see his lips moving as though he is in a deep conversation but he sits by himself. Is this why purple eyes are abominations? It makes us act weird? But why aren't I affected?

I read the page again. Acting weird? Wesley hasn't gone insane. It can't be the eyes that is making Adrian go crazy. Perhaps it is the isolation? I flip to the next page.

Last night he woke me up, screaming for something to get out of his head. He was asleep when he was screaming this but I couldn't wake him.

I then woke up this morning to him watching me, murmuring something under his breath.

It's almost sunset and I am still down by the waterfall. I am too scared to return to our new home, and I can't go back to our old one. Adrian hasn't spoken to me or touched me in almost a week. When he does look at me, he has an insane

*look in his eyes. I'm scared. He always has a weapon on him,
even when he sleeps. It's like he's paranoid and it's almost
like he is looking at me as the enemy. I need to break our
bond; he isn't the boy I've known my whole life.*

I hear him calling, I must hide.

I turn the page again, getting lost into the words.

*He didn't find me last night, though I could hear him
calling me until the sun began to rise. I was too scared to
sleep but my eyes were barely staying open. I am also
freezing; I'm hiding in the caves behind the water of the
waterfall. I am soaked and cold, I'm surprised I am not sick
yet. I'm going to try and sleep, I need to be on my best game.*

My heart is racing in my chest, I am nervous for this
girl. I dread what the next page is going to bring.

*I finally braved returning home to Adrian. He was
sitting in front of the fire when I arrived, a knife in his hand.
He was twirling it on his palm, into it, blood falling into the
dirt at his feet. I went to him to take the knife from him but
he attacked me. I managed to avoid the knife by falling
backwards, I pushed myself up from the ground and ran,
into the forest. I reached the cliffs, I had gone the wrong way.
I begged him to stop and not come any closer. But he
attacked me again. Instinctively I threw my hands up but a
force of energy blew from my body like a small grenade and
threw Adrian backwards and off the cliff.*

The next few pages have been torn out. The book is

old. But this girl knew Nicholas. Have there been two runaways in Bellator tribe? There were only five years between Nicholas and I, how do I not know of this girl? I must ask Wesley or Sierra. My mind strains to think back, irritating me that I can't remember.

"It was a cover up," I say to myself, and I remember hearing my dad talk about a young boy from Bellator who died in a freak accident near the waterfalls. *Freak accident, freak hunting trip.* Every time something happened, they cover up the truth. What else are the islands leaders hiding from us?

I notice within the ripped-out pages is one that is just folded. I open it, her handwriting on this page almost unreadable.

I can hear them. With their swords and pitchforks. They come to find the monster in the woods. The one that killed their precious gold boy. Perhaps I did kill Adrian. Perhaps I made him jump. Maybe I have been the monster all along.

They are coming.

It was an accident. In this bed, alone, I miss him.

They are coming.

I am not an abomination.

They are coming.

I hear them.

They are close.

They are coming.

I feel my mind maddening.

Is it from the isolation?

Is it from this power within me?

Are purple eyes truly cursed?

They are coming.
They are here.

I'm fixated on the words, drawn into the diary, when someone taps me on the shoulder. Fear sparking the magic from me, a force of energy blows out of me. For a moment my vision blurs in front of my eyes and a weird vibrating sensation covers my skin, I struggle to breathe as though I have just run a few miles and my mind is spinning, trying to focus on what happened. I turn away and see Sierra laying on the floor unconscious. I run to her and try to wake her. She doesn't respond.

Chapter Thirteen

I run into the medical centre behind two Bellators that are carrying Sierra. They showed up when they heard me shouting for help.

I try to run into the room with them but I am stopped at the door by a middle age Lex woman. Her brunette hair is pulled back into a ponytail and her circle glasses rest upon her nose. I see her lips moving, but I can't hear what she is saying. I am trying to see into the room.

"What happened?" the Lex woman asks, placing her hand on my arm.

I open my mouth but no words come out. I don't know what to say, I don't know how to explain what happened because I don't understand myself. The words from the diary haunt me. Maybe I have been the monster all along.

From behind me I hear footsteps, and I turn to see my parents running towards me. My father bursts into the room, but my mother runs to my side and embraces me. She pulls me away from the Lex woman who turns away and enters the room to talk to my father.

"What happened?" my mother asks me in a hushed whisper.

I begin to cry and claim that it was an accident. She pulls me in for another hug and says she isn't mad and doesn't blame me.

"I should have known this was your fault!" states a voice. Mum releases me and I look up at Lord Mason. "You almost killed your sister! You're a monster!"

"Don't talk to my daughter like that!" snaps my father, exiting the room my sister is in. He turns to me. "She is going to be fine."

My mother lets her hand fall beside me, and embraces it. I squeeze it, and her support flows through me, keeping me strong from crying more.

"You're still banished from this island," Lord Mason says venomously. He then turns to my parents. "I understand that she is your daughter, but she has brought nothing but destruction since she returned to the island. She is an abomination."

I grab my father's hand, silencing him from saying anything. The fact that he changed his mind and decided to support me means everything to me.

"I want to see my sister before I leave," I say, keeping my eyes down.

Lord Mason scoffs. I look up and meet his gaze. He

gives me two minutes and walks back down the hall. I release my parents' hands and walk into the room. I hear them follow me in as I stand before Sierra's bed. She just looks like she is sleeping, peaceful. According to the medics, I knocked her unconscious and she should wake up in a few hours, they are just monitoring her blood pressure and brain waves to ensure no further harm was inflicted. Dad stands behind me, with his hand around my shoulder, whilst Mum goes and sits by the side.

I apologise but my father hushes me.

"I am sorry," he says. I look up at him, and he looks down at his feet. "That I made you feel like you needed to run away when this happened to you. And I am sorry for how I reacted when you came home."

I hug him and whisper that I love him.

I step out of his hug and ask him for all the details he knows about the Bellator boy who died a few years ago and Nicholas's death.

He looks confused at the question but he answers.

"The Bellator boy ran away with his girlfriend; everyone assumed they had bonded. The town was told it was an accident, he fell into a waterfall. But I saw the body, it was mutated, I can't even begin to explain what I think happened to that boy."

He looks out the window, as though he is remembering back to that day. I break his concentration and ask about Nicholas.

"Nicholas loved to hunt, every month he would go out for a few days. This time, a week had passed and he hadn't returned so Lord Mason sent men out and they found his body."

It's interesting information and neither confirms nor disproves my belief that this is a cover-up. Thanking Dad for the information, I tell them I have to leave, as my two minutes are probably about to end.

"You're not leaving again are you?" Mum asks, looking up from Sierra's bed.

I shake my head and put my forefinger to my lips, and I wink at them both before exiting the room. I see Lord Mason at the end of the hallway, I give him a little wave as a sarcastic motion before turning away and walking out of the medical centre.

Chapter Fourteen

My skin is a shade of pink from being in the sun for too long. I sit on a fallen tree, out of sight, in the clearing. The water is blue and clear, it's mesmerising, as though the sand below the waves is made of diamonds. The Piscator Tribe are at work, some working on the beach. Their skin is golden from being outdoors all day, their blue eyes shining like beacons. A few of the workers are red, raw, showing that they are new to the tribe, from another. A dark-haired boy I recognise runs onto the sand and wolf-called, a signal. The boats are returning.

The more experienced of the tribe would go fish or collect supplies from other islands, though from the size of the boats returning I am assuming the latter. The last time I saw this dark-haired boy, his eyes were still grey and he was barely double digits in age, and now, if it wasn't tribe before family, I could call him a brother-in-law. He is Tahlia's younger brother. Ethan looks to be late teens now. Women and men run out into the crystal-clear waters and are thrown ropes from those on the boats. They pull the boats into the shallows and tie them to the holding post. An older gentleman steps off the boat and into the shallows, walking up to another elder gentleman who has been sitting at a table writing god knows what since I've been here watching. The gentleman from the boat has grey hair that is just visible below his captains' hat, his poet shirt almost see-through from being splashed by the water. He leans down to the man at the table, whose glasses sits on the edge of his nose. He looks up with a smile, pleased by the news his captain is telling him.

I watch as tribe members from the boats hand crates to those in the water. They are careful not to allow the water to caress the boxes as they bring them onto shore. These crates look different to the ones usually brought aboard. The crates are usually opened, not sealed. I stand as I watch Ethan take a box up to the two elder men. He uses a crowbar to open the crate and takes something out of the box to show them. I stand on my tip toes trying to see what is in the box but I can't get a clear view. The two elder men nod their approval to Ethan then stand, taking the box with them when they walk away.

Walking out of the trees, I call out to Ethan once I know the two elders are out of earshot. He turns and smiles when he sees me. He glances around to ensure no one else heard me before approaching. I take a step back into the trees and out of sight from the rest of the tribe.

"I heard you were in town. Apparently you let wolves loose to ruin Nicholas's funeral," he says with a childish smirk as he reaches me. "I was also told not to speak to you."

He finds my eyes and loses the smile, nodding as though he now understands why I am to be avoided at all cost. Surprising me, he doesn't walk away; he asks why I called him over. Glad he isn't asking other questions, I also go straight to the point and ask what was in the crates.

"A serum," he says bluntly. Suppressing an eye roll at male communication, I ask what the serum is for. "It's to break the bond between people. The Lex tribe has been working on it for years. They believe that we should make our own choice, tribe wise and lover wise."

Hiding my shock at the truth of the serum, I ask Ethan what he believes.

"I like things how they are. I love who fate put me with, and if I was given a choice, I would probably have too much fear to leave my family's tribe. But now that I am here, I would have it no other way."

He reaches into his back pocket and pulls out two vials full with soft blue liquid. He hands them both to me. I hold out my hand to accept. "Just in case you're not happy with the choice fate gave you, you both need to drink the vial."

"Will my eyes return to grey?" I ask, holding the

vials before me.

He shrugs. "The Lex were working on a way to make your eyes change once you make your own choice, but if they've put this in the serum or even worked it out, we have no idea. We are just their delivery sluts."

"Why are you telling me this? You could get in a lot of trouble."

Ethan looks over his shoulder, then turns back to me.

"You seem like someone that will always do what is right, despite the consequences. The Lex believe they can control us and everything around them. They use this island as a play thing. I don't agree with it."

I thank Ethan, and he smiles at me and turns away, walking back down to his tribe. My eyes fall down to the vials that still reside in my hand. Could this actually work? I want to break the bond between Wesley and I, but a part of me doesn't want to lose the purple. It is a part of me now. I close my hand around the vials and hold them protectively. I have a choice to make. I walk away from the sandy ground and back to the dirt. I can only hope I have my mind made up by the time I reach Wesley's house.

Chapter Fifteen

Scaling the tree outside the front of the Mason house probably isn't the smartest move, but it is definitely a better choice than knocking on the front door and risking Lord Mason answering.

I edge my way along the branch and step forward, climbing through the open window; it is Nicholas's room. It's exactly how I remember it: the red bed sheets, the weapons on the wall, the books in the corner. I walk over to the door and slip out; the hallway is empty. I walk down to the next door, open it, and step inside the room.

Wesley sits up from his bed when he sees it is me. I have the vials in my back pocket. I walk over and sit beside him.

"They had a town meeting the other night. Dad knows you're still here and wants to send a hunting party out for you," he says. I ask what the verdict was with his dad's word against me. "The majority of the town decided the wolves were a bigger risk, so the Bellator are currently hunting them, though how, I am not sure."

We sit in silence for a few minutes, neither of us willing to say anything. My eyes fixate on the spiral patterns in the carpet.

"You need to let me go," I say, breaking the silence. I feel him turn to look at me but I keep my eyes trained to the ground. "I was gone, for seven years. I kept my thoughts and emotions to myself. If you had let me go, we would no longer be bonded."

I am not sure if that is true, but I have to believe it is, and I need him to believe it. I look over at him, and give him a small smile.

"We bonded because fate thought we belonged together," he argues. "We can't just decide to break what fate wanted."

"Actually, we can," I say looking at him. He turns to meet my gaze, confused. "We didn't bond because we belonged together. We bonded so I could evolve. You are just fate's victim in allowing me to achieve my potential."

Wesley looks away from me and we fall into silence. I can hear his mind at war with itself, but I tune out, allowing him to process without me tuning in.

"Kiss me goodbye?" he asks.

I look from his eyes to his lips. I close my eyes and lean forward, softly caressing his lips. It is the softest, gentlest kiss, not filled with passion, but affection, sadness and loss.

"I miss my best friend," I whisper, my lips still inches from his. I lean back and open my eyes. I feel sad, wishing I did love him. He gives me a small smile and we fall back into silence.

I feel it is over. I tune in to see if he feels the same when I realise, I can't feel his heartbeat anymore. I look at him. He is looking out the window. My hand goes to the side of his face and turns his head to look at me.

I let out a laugh.

"Your eyes," he says, tilting his head to see better. "They've changed; it's like the purple has become more vibrant."

I smile at him, and bite my lower lip slightly.

"And your eyes are grey again."

Chapter Sixteen

It's the third morning that Sierra has been in the medical centre. I always visit at sunrise because no one but nurses are around.

I hold a bunch of sunflowers in my hand. Yellow, vibrant, and freshly cut from a Terra field. The hallway is bare, no windows, no art, just white walls and circular lights on the ceiling. I turn into room fourteen with a forced smile on my face. But the room is empty, the bed stripped of its sheets, the window blinds closed.

I step back into the hallway. Deserted. Not a medic in sight. The medical centre is run by a mixture of Lex and Terra tribe, which was how I grew up so close to Nicholas and Wesley.

Their mother and mine work here.

Looking around again, I call out a hello which

echoes through the hallways. Fear consumes my chest and I can't shake the feeling that something is wrong. I try and reason with my brain that I am being paranoid, but I can't erase that nagging feeling in my stomach that something isn't right. That's when I notice the green light bleeding under a door at the far end of the hallway. I take off in a run towards the door and slam it open and enter the room. Lord Mason and others I don't recognise stand in an antechamber sort of viewing area that looks in on an operating theatre through a window. Though currently all eyes are on me.

I notice in the other room two occupied gurneys. One with Tahlia and the other with Sierra.

Rage fills me and I go to run forward but two Bellator men grab my arms and hold me back.

"What are you doing to my sister?" I demand.

Lord Mason turns to me and holds out a vial of blue liquid. Like the one I almost gave to his son. "We haven't had a chance to test these," he explains. "If something goes wrong or they die–"

"You're going to blame me?" I interrupt, my heart racing in my chest, realising the reality of trouble I've brought on my sister by returning home. Lord Mason makes a comment about me being an abomination and goes back to watching the experiment. I see two men inject a vial into Sierra and Tahlia's veins. I can't let this happen! I slam my heel into the foot of one of the men holding me. From the pain I cause his grip on me loosen, giving me the chance to elbow him in the stomach. He hurls over, releasing me completely. I turn to slam the palm of my hand into the nose of the other man holding me. He lets go, both his hands going to his nose. I glance at the other men in the room, daring them to stop me, but all keep their distance.

I shove open the door to the other room and run to my sister. I stroke her hairline gently and say her name. She blinks, scrunches her face as though she's in pain. Her eyes are still green which makes me relax a little. She sits up and starts coughing, she covers her mouth as the coughs get more violent. She manages to stop coughing but her breathing is heavy, when she removes her hand away from her mouth, I notice blood on her hand. I panic and ask if she is okay but she cries that it hurts. When I ask what hurts and she cries, "Everything." She starts scratching at her skin as though something is beneath it. All of a sudden, she freezes and looks at me with a look of shock in her eyes. "I can't hear anything," she whispers. I ask her what she means and she turns to Tahlia. "It's gone."

I realise she means the bond. I turn to look at Tahlia, who is waking up. When her eyes blink open, I notice her eyes are red. She doesn't look to be in pain. She sits up and looks through the window at Lord Mason. He walks in and approaches Tahlia. Whispers words such as *magnificent*. I suddenly feel very nervous, I don't trust Lord Mason and what else he has planned but I am not going to stick around to find out. I whisper to Sierra that we should go, and I help her from her bed. She leans on me for support. When Lord Mason takes a step towards me and states that

I'm not leaving, I throw forward a wave of energy that halts everyone in their spot. I half drag, half carry Sierra out of the room and down the corridor. It feels like time is going in slow motion but I'm moving as fast as I can. As soon as the automatic doors to the medical centre open, I call for help but no one appears.

I hear screaming from behind me, and I turn to see the medical centre has gone up in flames. Fearing for Tahlia, and what losing her completely would do to Sierra, I lower her to the ground. My instinct takes over as I run towards it, but it is too late, the flame must have hit the gas lines because the whole building explodes, throwing me backwards. I groan in pain as I land and roll over to look at the ruins left of the building. I don't understand what happened? How did the building catch fire? Why did the flame spread so fast? I look over my shoulder back at Sierra. How am I going to tell her?

I crawl over to Sierra and put her arm around me, and help her stand. We walk through town and through the trees and down to the beach. I sigh in relief to see my boat is still there. I put her in the boat and explain that it is going to take her to a friend that will help her.

"Where is Tahlia?" she asks. Struggling to stay conscious. I hear voices further down the beach. I tell Sierra to wait for a moment. I race down the reach and see the Piscators, I sigh in relief when I see Ethan. I call out to him and he walks over to me, I take him to Sierra. I explain that the boat is enchanted to take him to a friend of mine but I need him to look after Sierra.

"What happened to her?" he asks. I tell him how Lord Mason used her and Tahlia as test subjects for the vial he had given me.

He curses and asks where Tahlia is. Unable to answer him, especially in front of Sierra, I tell him I will go find out. He thanks me and gets in the boat. I push the boat in the water and watch it sail away. Anxiety and worry for my sister scratches at my chest and up into my throat. I hope that Lucian can help her.

I run back through the trees, back to the medical centre, but there is still no one here. Where are the Bellator Tribe?

"You took your time," says a voice behind me.

I turn around and my heart almost stops. Nicholas is leaning on a tree, smiling at me. His red eyes flick between me and the fire. His hair is shorter, and his muscles have doubled. His tanned skin is now covered in scars and tattoos that were not there when I knew him before.

Registering what he said to me, I ask if it was him who blew up the medical centre. He smirks as he pushes back from the tree and starts walking over to me. I feel a chill at his lack of response and I know.

"But your father was in there!" I protest.

He shrugs as though he has no care in the world. When he reaches me, he grabs me and pulls me into a kiss. For a moment I am sixteen again, when I loved kissing this boy. But that was many moons ago. I am not that girl and he is not that boy. I push back from him and he makes a childish comment about missing me.

"My sister was in there, if I hadn't gotten her out-"
I slap him across the face, and he just laughs. I stare at
him, horrified.

"Whose body did we all mourn over at the burial?"
I ask.

He shrugs and walks past me over to the rubble.
He kicks some rubble toward the still-roaring block-
sized fire of the medical centre as if it were just a
campfire he could snuff out. Was he always this
arrogant?

"Why aren't the Bellator tribe here? They are meant
to protect the island!"

He smirks, and makes a comment about causing a
distraction on the other side of the island. He
continues to say we should get out of here because the
Bellator tribe will show up eventually and throw us
both in a cell.

"For fuck's sake, Nicholas! I am going to get the
blame for this!" I curse.

"I hope so," he states, as he walks past me and into
the trees. I turn around to watch him walk back
through the trees.

I take a look around and decide to follow him. I
want to know what his game is. He faked his own
death for a reason; he is up to something.

Chapter Seventeen

He walks through the forest, continually looking around to make sure no one is following, but I keep my distance far enough so that I am out of sight. As we venture further into the forest, I realise I know this place. Not from being here before, but from the diary. It's as she described it. This is the waterfall that she had hid in when her mate was going insane. I look ahead and see that Nicholas is almost out of view. I quickly follow after as he disappears over the top of the hill. When I reach the top, I am expecting to see the old worn-out cottage built by Adrian and the diary girl, but there are multiple little cottages, new and well built.

That's when I see her, another girl with purple eyes. But that's not the only reason I can't take my eyes off her. Her brunette hair falls down in loose curls, her eyes a vibrant violet, decorated with black liner and golden powder. I can't help but feel a powerful attraction towards her, my skin flushes as my mind runs wild. As I walk down from where I hide to the cottages, she notices me. She looks at me with the same magnetism as I feel looking at her.

Karlson and Ella, the people I saw with Wesley, are practising their archery behind her. But they stop and walk to stand behind her when they notice me, as though protecting her if anything happens. When Nicholas notices them all looking behind him, he stops and turns around.

He says something as I reach him but my eyes are focused on hers. I pause my infatuation for a moment to realise how weird it is seeing purple eyes on someone else.

"You thought you were the only one?" she asks me as I stop before her. "I'm Lydia."

She offers her hand, and I go to accept but Nicholas clears his throat. I turn away from her and look at him. From behind me I hear Karlson ask Lydia what she would like him to do.

"Nothing," she replies softly. "She is free to go as she pleases."

Nicholas turns to Lydia with his smoulder look and asks her to have me stay awhile. Anger fills me, I turn to Ella and summon her bow and an arrow to me. I point aim at Nicholas, sidestepping so Lydia and the other two aren't behind me.

Nicholas turns his charming smile on me. "You won't do that."

His arrogance will be the death of him.

"Dare me," I snarl.

Lydia takes a step forward, but she's not foolish enough to stand dead between us. She lingers to the side and suggests that I lower my weapon and that Nicholas walk away.

"What even happened to you?" I snap at him, ignoring Lydia. "You killed your own father! And what about your mum or Wesley? They mourned you!"

"Well, it's a good thing he had you to comfort him, isn't it, Amity? You hear I'm dead and you coming running back to him. When you fucked him did you wish it was me?"

I pull on the string of my bow, getting ready to release. Lydia now moves to stand between Nicholas and I. Obviously she knows I am not bluffing.

"I knew!" he fumed. "I knew your eyes would change to purple when you bonded. I wanted it, but you bonded with my twat of a brother."

I falter, and lower the arrow, looking at Nicholas questioningly. How could he know my eyes would change purple? I laugh in bitter realisation, remembering times that I spent with Nicholas.

"They used to flicker, didn't they?" I ask. He nods at me. I scoff. "Well, I am no longer bonded with your brother, and for the longest time, I wished I had bonded with you. Because I loved you. I would have suggested we run away together, perhaps then you would have gotten yourself thrown off a cliff."

Lydia looks at me, as though surprised that I have

actually read the diary.

"You didn't answer my question?" Nicholas smirked as arrogance dripped off his lips. "Did you think of me when you were with Wes?"

I raise the arrow again and this time I don't hesitate to release it. It buries itself in his shoulder.

He grunts in pain and curses me, "I wish you were in the medical centre when I blew it up."

Lydia ordered Karlson to take Nicholas inside to look at his injury.

As Karlson reaches Nicholas I ask him why he blew up the medical centre.

"It was the only way to get our hands on that serum," he says. "The Lex tribe has most of it locked up in their building, but the medical centre is much easier to get into to."

Disgust fills me. I drop the bow and ran my hands back through my hair. I am horrified at the man Nicholas had grown into. I remember the boy I loved, the boy that used to push me on the swing set. It is all tainted now.

I feel a racing heartbeat in my chest. It isn't mine, it isn't Wesley's. It is Sierra. I can feel her fighting for her life. I remember Wesley saying my eyes had gone brighter after we unbonded - did my magic evolve? I cough, a ghost cough I feel from Sierra, and slowly, unbelievably, impossibly, I feel her life force fade in my chest.

Anger flashes through me, followed by tearing agony.

"For the record, Nicholas," I fume. "I never fucked

your brother."

As I turn away, Lydia runs forward and asks where I am going. For a moment I don't plan on answering her.

"Before Nicholas blew up the medical centre, his father used the serum on my sister and her mate. It killed her, and now I am going to destroy it and anyone that gets in my way."

Before anyone can say anything, I take off into the forest, as fast as my legs will take me. Tears falling down my face, blurring my vision as I run.

Chapter Eighteen

I should have gone to my parents to tell them but I am too focused on destroying the serum. I run to the Mason house. I walk up to the front door and start banging my fist until Wesley opens the door.

He opens his mouth to say something but I push past him and walk through the house. I stop in the doorway of the kitchen when I hear Lord and Lady Mason arguing. How is he alive?

"Why are you still hunting her?" I hear Lady Mason demand.

"Because she is a monster and must be eliminated. You saw what she did to the medical centre!"

"You don't know that was her!" she defends me. "Her magic could be useful."

Lord Mason states that they have warriors that do their job well enough and storms out of the kitchen.

When I am sure he was gone, I enter, with Wesley at my back.

"Do you really believe I am not a monster?" I ask. She jumps but then turns and looks at me without fear in her eyes, just resignation of the girl she knew years ago. She nods and looks out the door that her husband left through.

"Nicholas is still alive."

"What?" Wesley demands of us.

I tell Lady Mason what her husband did to my sister, and she's shocked and angry. I tell her I need to get into Lex Headquarters to find the serum and destroy it. She agrees to help me. As we go to leave, I turn to Wesley.

"I always remember your dad and Nicholas arguing because they could never share an opinion. It's funny that the first thing they agree on is murdering me."

Wesley argues that I am wrong, he buried his brother, he saw his body. He chooses not to believe me, because believing me is accepting that his brother and father are not who he knew them to be.

Lady Mason turns to me and asks if it's true that I bonded with Nicholas. I glance to Wesley before I tell her the truth. But I ensure her that the bond has been broken so Wesley is unbonded again. Lady Mason pulls out a blank, silver card and hands it to me. As I accept it, she explains that its an electronic key that will give me access through any doors in the Lex Headquarters. I tell her thanks, and with a quick glance at Wesley, I exit the house out the back door and walk the back paths through the forest to Lex Headquarters. I walk through the forest, hoping I am going the correct way. I have an idea of where headquarters should be, but I've never actually been there.

I hear a wolf in the distance; stopping in my tracks, I listen. I am being hunted. Through the trees I see a Bellator hunting party, but from somewhere far back from behind me I can hear the wolves.

I leave the path and run through the forest. I can hear the wolves howling, getting louder. My legs are starting to get stiff from running. I make a mental note to start doing morning runs if I get out of this alive. *IF* I get out of this alive. I run into a clearing where dozen Bellators greet me.

"Stand down!" one of them shouts. "If you do not come with us, we will use deadly force to make you comply."

I ask where they plan to take me, and he tells me the cells in the Lex headquarters. I weigh my options. If I surrender myself, I get away from Nicholas and the wolves as well as being placed in the exact location I am heading towards.

Two of the men with red eyes step forward. I hold out my wrist, allowing them to cuff me. The younger of the two seems nervous, he keeps his eyes and head down, avoiding eye contact with me. But I see them glancing up, daring to peek under his blond hair. He must have bonded into the tribe. The other is tattooed, with brushed back, dark hair. He smirks as he cuffs me, and I notice his eyes study my body. I look up between the two of them and see Nicholas in the distance. I smirk at him as the Bellators turn me around and lead me in the direction of the Lex headquarters.

Chapter Nineteen

"How long do you plan to keep me here?" I ask the guard that is pacing back and forth in front of my cell. He looks familiar but I can't place where I know him from.

I glance around my cell; I am the only occupant. They mustn't arrest people much because there is one bed, in one small cubicle of a cell. I look back at the guard. He is keeping his eyes trained to the ground as he walks back and forth.

I murmur that his pacing is making me nervous. He stops in his tracks and looks at me, with his green eyes and red hair. I swear beneath my breath and look down, realising where I know him from.

"They don't know, do they?" I ask.

He looks towards the door, then turns back to me and takes a step towards the cell. Up close, I see freckles across his nose and cheeks. I remember seeing him as a young boy, always hiding behind his mother when they came over, always nose in a book instead of playing with Sierra and me.

"Where is Sierra?" he asks. I take a step back from the bars and cross my arms, refusing to answer. He sighs in frustration. "I am a friend of your family. Why would I hurt you or her?"

I hold up two fingers.

"Two reasons. One, I am an abomination. Two, it's tribe before family or friend or whatever and Sierra became a traitor the moment, I took her out of that hospital."

He scoffs and looks at the floor again. I can't for the life of me remember his name. As though reading my thoughts, he places his hands on the bars and leans on them and asks me if I even remember his name or his mother's. In truth I don't. His mum was my mother's friend, and we didn't have much to do with them except for the rare occasion they would visit the house.

"I thought so," he muses. "But oh, how I remember you, Amity Winters, the golden child, destined to bond with Nicholas Mason, become the new town mayor… and then what happened, you disappeared."

He leans forward, and I instinctively take a step back. He opens his mouth to say something else when a chaotic noise from the next room makes him stop. He turns towards the exit and tells me to stay where I am before going to investigate.

"I'm in a cage, how do you expect me to move?"

That's when I get the idea. I focus my energy on the lock and it blasts open. I run in the opposite direction of the commotion. Remembering what I came here to do, I run down to the main lobby and find the floor chart. I curse when I see that the lab is near the lock-up room so I can't get back up there.

The guards at the front door notice me. I run into the staircase, locking the door behind me, hoping it buys me time. I start running up the stairs, reminding myself to do more cardio before I attempt something like this again. When I reach the fifth floor, I stop and take a quick breather. I hear the door at the bottom slam open. Cursing again, I run up the last flight of stairs and onto the roof. I lock that as well. Now what? I ask myself as I look around wondering how I am now meant to get off this roof. I run over to the edge and look down. It is too high to jump, but climbing down looks near impossible.

If I wasn't running for my life, perhaps I would melt into the beauty of the view. I stand on top of the Lex Headquarters building. It isn't a very tall building, but it gives enough height to just see over the edge of the trees. It is like a painting, green blending into the ocean blue which melts into the orange sunset sky.

My toes against the edge of the roof. I look down at the jump, contemplating the injury. It would possibly result in a something broken, definitely will result in scratches on the legs and arms and sprains. I can hear the commotion downstairs, it is getting louder, which means they are getting closer to the roof. I have no choice. I sit on the ledge and roll onto my stomach, my feet reaching for a ledge. I place my fingers in the cracks between bricks and start to climb down. Once I have made it perhaps three floors, I decide to drop the rest of the way. I push myself off the wall. I almost land on my feet, but lose balance and fall onto my hands and knees. My hands feel as though the have pins and needles, my knee feels as though it was grazed in the fall to the ground. I sit back and investigate. My hands are red as though they want to bleed, but no cut was made.

"You took long enough," says a voice, breaking my concentration. I look up and see Lydia standing before me.

Chapter Twenty

Her brunette curls are pulled away from her face and thrown up in a bun, and her eyes look more vibrant with her hair out of her face. She offers me her hand, and I accept. She pulls me to my feet then hands me a quiver of arrows and a bow, which I instinctively throw over my back.

"Well, well, an abomination, two abominations," says Lord Mason, as he and Nicholas approach us. He has an arrow aimed at us as he comes to a standstill, whilst Nicholas just twirls a knife on his finger.

I draw an arrow and aimed it at Lord Mason.

"I am the last person you want to be around, Archer Mason," I say venomously, deliberately using his first name to take away the formality and show I have no respect to him as my leader. "You killed Sierra, for a fucking science experiment."

He smirks at me before answering. "Tahlia is perfectly fine. Maybe you should have been quicker to get out of the building, I got out with Tahlia before the detonation went off."

I pull tighter on the bowstring, ready to release the arrow when Lord Mason releases his. Lucky for me, Lydia is quicker, she steps forward and creates a shield between us. Lord Mason's arrow ricochets off.

I look at Lydia, who tilts her head to the side. I read the signal and nod, looking back at Lord Mason and release the arrow. I'm satisfied to see him dodge as expected, though a real archer would have known that arrow was not intended to hit him.

I turn and run after Lydia who has already taken off, following her through the trees. I hear Nicholas and his father behind us. Lydia's shield must have fallen once we left. She leads me to a waterfall and we run through the rushing water into a cavern behind it. I stay near the entrance and listen, but they must have run in the other direction because there is no sign of them.

I sit on one of the cold damp rocks, bring my knees to my chest and rest my arms and head on them. Lydia asks if I am okay and I ignore her, too tired to reply. I have to go tell my parents that Sierra is dead. How do I tell them that?

Lydia approaches me and sits beside me on the rock. I feel my skin warm where her skin touches mine.

"Why did you come to the headquarters?" I ask her, tilting my head to meet her gaze.

She smiles at me, and says that she thought it was obvious.

I sit up, and shrug. Stretching my legs out, I let my hands fall down into my lap.

She reaches out her hand and entangles her fingers within mine. I feel a small spark ignite within our hands. I look at her, first her eyes, then my gaze falls down to her lips, which were trembling unexpectedly as she struggled to say something.

"I... I'm so sorry about your sister. This war they're waging on us should never have touched her. This whole thing - it isn't fair."

She leans forward tentatively and kisses me. I feel myself melt into the kiss, then my mind gets in the way. I wonder if this is what it was like for Sierra the first time she kissed Tahlia.

I break off the kiss and sit back, the full extent of the loss of Sierra settling in. I feel like a black hole has been formed where my heart is, and I'm just getting pulled into it. Guilt ravishes me, for if I had never come home, Sierra would still be alive. I need to make Lord Mason pay for this.

"There will be a town meeting tonight, I need you to get Nicholas there," I say to Lydia before standing up and walking to the mouth of the waterfall.

I stop and turn back, meeting Lydia's gaze. I feel that magnetism again.

"I hope I am not wrong in trusting you."

I exit the waterfall and walk through the forest and towards town. Tonight, everything ended. First stop is my parents' house: they need to know. When I reach their house, our house, I walk up, suppressing my nerves. I knock twice on the door. My Mum answers and embraces me in a hug. I take her into the living room and call for Dad. When he comes in, I ask them both to sit.

I stand before them, lost for words. Not knowing what to say, I pull the serum bottles out of my back pocket and hand them to Mum. She asks what they are.

"They break bonds. Lord Mason gave it to Sierra and Tahlia. It killed Sierra."

Mum starts crying, Dad looks broken and shocked. He demands me to explain everything I know.

I tell how about the beach when I got the serum and tell him everything that happened in the medical centre that day.

"I need to confront Lord Mason about it, have the whole town know who he is."

Dad confirms that there has been a town meeting called this evening. I ask Mum if she can find needles for us to use the serum at the meeting.

Chapter Twenty-One

As the town gathers, I hide in the back, a wig and hat upon my head, eyes down. Sitting beside my parents. The seats are divided to both sides of the hall, with a pathway in the middle. When the meeting starts Lord Mason goes to the podium at the front and starts by thanking everyone for coming.

"I have called you all here tonight because there is a danger on the island. Amity Winters is still here. This girl has blown up our medical centre, caused damage to expensive equipment within Lex Headquarters building and attempted to murder me. Something has to be done."

I stand up from where I am seated and move to the aisle.

"Why don't you tell them how you killed my sister?" I say, removing my hat and wig, throwing them to the floor. Everyone gasps. I hear whispers, asking when Sierra died and if it was true. "Your leader here," I say, pointing to him as I walk down the aisle towards him. "He created this serum, if injected it breaks a bond. However, there is a catch: if you don't want the bond broken, it kills you, like it did my sister."

Lies!

Abomination!

She probably killed her sister!

Knowing the town would turn on me, I remove the serum from my jacket, in its needles, ready to be injected.

"Don't believe me?" I muse. "Does anyone wish to volunteer?"

To my surprise Lady Mason stands up and offers for her and her husband to be injected. Lord Mason looks from me to his wife, fuming.

I walk over to Lady Mason and inject her with the serum. I hand her the other needle for her to inject her husband. Afterwards, we wait and watch. Kirstin Mason's eyes don't change, but her husband Archer, his eyes fade from green to red.

Turning back to the town, not hiding my victory smile.

"What does this mean?" Wesley asks. "Are my parents still bonded?"

I shake my head, retrieving the empty serum needles from Lady Mason. I hold them up for the room to see.

"This serum, it completely breaks the bond. Before

my sister died, she cried that she couldn't feel anything. She lost the complete connection to Tahlia." Lowering my arm, I continue. "Want to know what else your leader has been doing? Lying about the death of his son."

This statement causes an uproar. I hear the word liar and abomination shouted out. But as though fate is on my side, the door opens, and Nicholas comes flying through the door while Lydia and Ella walk gracefully up the stairs and through the door.

Whispers from their tribes begin. From the words I catch, they all assumed them both to be dead.

Nicholas looks up and sees me. He grabs a knife from the Bellator boy sitting near him and lunges at me. I draw my sword but before I can attack, an arm grabs me and pull the sword from my grip, I turn and am shocked to see it's Wesley. He stands before me, holding my own sword against me.

"Wesley! What are you doing?" I exclaim, completely baffled.

"He is my brother," is all he can say, but I can see a battle being waged in his head.

Chapter Twenty-Two

An arrow flies past me and imbeds itself into Wesley's shoulder. He screams out in pain and stumbles backwards, releasing the sword. I turn to see who my knight in shining armour is. To my surprise I see Lucian standing in the door frame.

I open my mouth to ask how and when but as though reading my mind he answers before I can ask.

"I got a boat after I buried your sister."

"Lucian?" Kirstin Mason murmurs softly. He stops in his tracks and his facial expression shows he is confused.

"I thought you were dead," he says.

As I begin to ask what is going on, Lord Mason grabs me and holds a knife to my throat. He stands close behind me so there is no wiggle room out of the knife. Lucian threatens him to release me. I question and demand what is going on, very aware of the cold blade against my skin. He presses the knife harder against my throat that I fear even breathing will cause my skin to break under the blade. My heart is thumping so loud in my ears, and it's the only sound, the room has fallen silent. Watching every second of drama unfolding within the room.

"Let me tell you a story about your friend Lucian there," Lord Mason snarls. "You see he used to be a part of this island. But he was like you, an abomination. The whole town saw how his bond mate went insane. After she died, my loving wife was there for him, comforted him, next thing you know, I have two sons. Now how is that possible, since I am unable to have children?"

The murmuring in the room is stilled into deep shock. Wesley and Nicholas look at each other, as startled as everyone else to realise they've never been who they thought they were. Lucian is *their father* - not the awful man who has persecuted my whole adult life. I wonder whether this was why I was so ready to adopt Lucian as my foster father on that island.

"Lucian?" I question.

He doesn't hear me though, which hurts. His gaze is focused on Lord Mason, rage consuming his features. He raises his bow again, an arrow aimed at Lord Mason. He demands to know why he told him that Lady Mason had died in childbirth.

"She belonged to me and only me!" Lord Mason shouts.

I stomp my heel into Lord Mason's foot, he grunts in pain and I elbow him in the ribs. I wince as the knife nicks my skin, so I grab it and twist it from his hand. I turn and punch him in the nose.

"That was for Sierra."

I turn and walk to Lucian; he takes his focus from Lord Mason to me and lowers his bow. I ask him to take me home.

"You're leaving?" Mum asks. I turn and see her standing in the crowd, looking at me with tears in her eyes. I nod, my heart breaking at leaving her again. She turns away from me and leaves the building, Dad looks at me before following her out.

I look at Wesley and Nicholas, confused with what I feel. I turn away from both of them and walk past them and out of the hall.

Epilogue

Everything on the island has changed.

Half the island is lining up to get the serum to separate from their bond mate. The other half is protesting it.

Kirstin packs her bags and gets on a boat with Lucian back to our little island.

My parents are hurt that I chose to leave them again. I tried to reach out before leaving the island but neither wanted to see me.

Wesley and Nicholas are reconnected, but I avoid both of them. As Lucian's sons, I feel like they're more my family than ever, and yet I even when I ran away I never felt as unsure about my future with either of them.

The whole island is in an uproar about who the new leaders of the town should be, the Mason family name blacklisted. As well as the Winters name. Not that it matters – both lines are effectively ended. One night can change everything.

I stand on the cliff overlooking the ocean, looking at Thira from a distance, wondering if I should have never left in the first place. Returning home has only made everything worse.

"Amity."

I turn around to see who had said my name and see Lydia standing before me, her brunette curls blowing in the wind. She walks towards me and stops a few feet in front of me.

Her eyes flash silver, and from the smile she is giving me, I know mine have changed as well.

Also by Danica Peck

www.ingramcontent.com/pod-product-compliance
Lightning Source LLC
Chambersburg PA
CBHW030436120726
47903CB00003B/995